Light in the Darkness

by Lesa Cline-Ransome

Illustrations by James E. Ransome

 JUMP AT THE SUN BOOKS

New York

"Rosa."

In the dark of our cabin I can't see my mama, but I can feel her breath on my face in whispers.

"It's time."

I rise from my pallet on the floor and stumble. Mama holds my hand tight and pulls me close. "Follow me," she says, even softer.

For Stephanie Owens Lurie:
Again, thank you for your patience, guidance,
and wisdom in bringing my words to life

—L.C-R.

Dedicated to the light in my life, Lesa

—J.R.

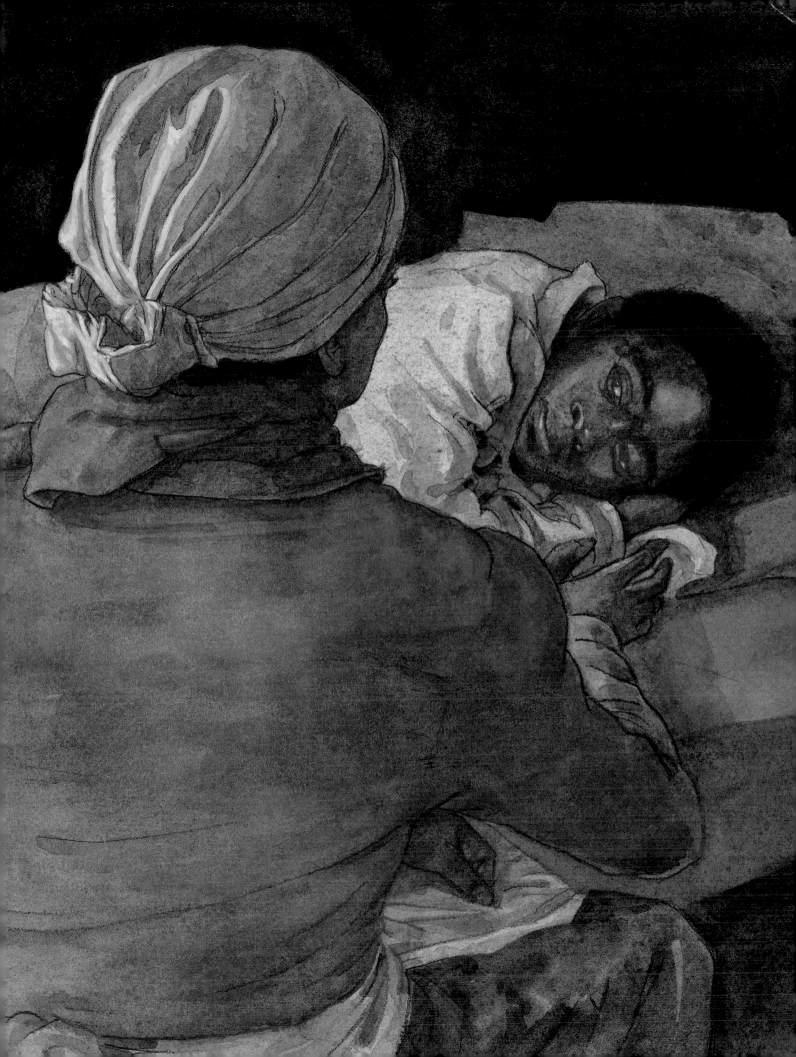

I hurry, because now I know where we are going. I grab
the back of Mama's skirt and stay close, following her
steps as best I can out of our cabin and into the night.
Most everyone in the quarter is asleep, but we still crouch
low and walk with soft steps till we reach the field.

We have to make sure the patrollers don't catch us and
take us to Master. We carry the darkness with us out
of the quarter, through the trees, down past the creek.
When Mama stops, I stop. When Mama turns, I turn.
Our walk is long and silent, and broken twigs and sharp
rocks cut the bottoms of our feet.

One night last week, when the lantern was out and the cabin was cool, Mama told me about a place we could go to learn letters.

"Like the letters Morris reads to us from the Bible on Sunday?" I asked her.

"Just like those," Mama said.

Mama says down the road a bit, at the Pompey plantation, the master's wife taught Morris to read the Bible when he was young. Guess she never figured he'd take that learning and make a school. He's old now, but he held on to his learning long enough to teach us.

Mama says one day, when we're free, we're gonna need those letters. But for now we have to act like reading is the last thing we want to do. Master once whipped a slave girl who learned to read. We all had to watch him give her a lash for every letter she learned. Mama stepped in front of me so I couldn't see, but I could still hear the whip.

Tonight we walk till my legs feel like they can't walk anymore.

Mama stops and whispers, "Here."

She calls out like a bird, then the bushes in front of us move to the side. We step forward and look down into a big hole in the ground. In the light of a lantern I see faces, young and old, looking up at us. As many as the fingers on my hands. Some of the faces I know, and some I don't.

Arms reach up to help us down. First me, then Mama. We squeeze into the center of a pit barely big enough for us to stand in. Branches move back into place, making a roof that pricks our hair.

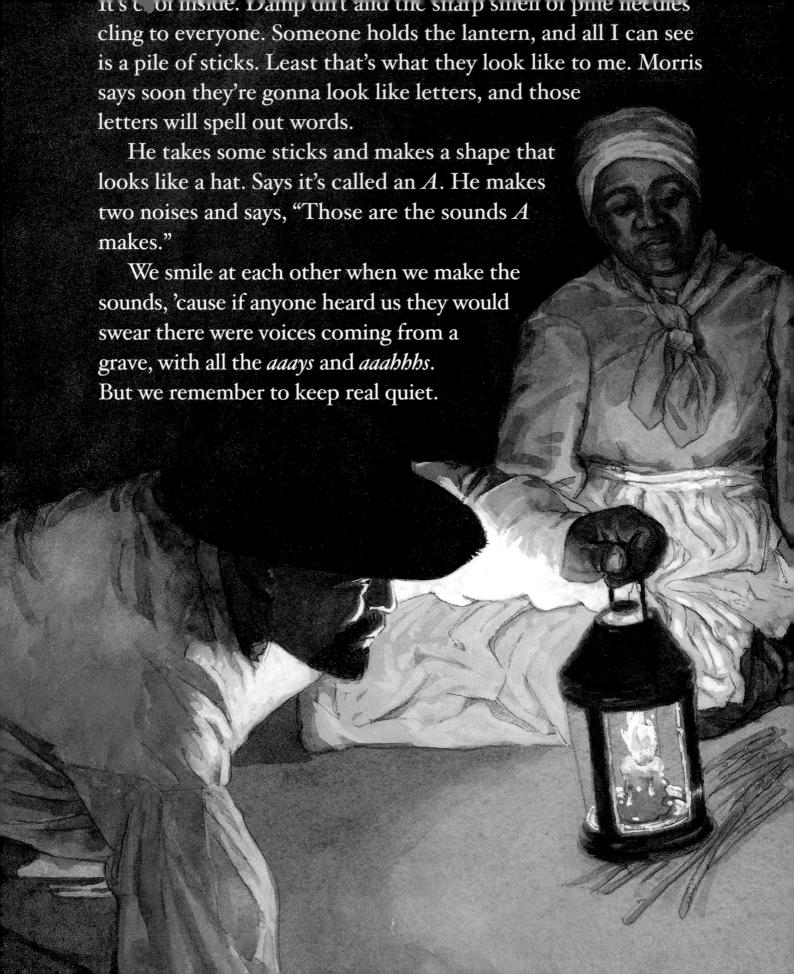

It's cool inside. Damp dirt and the sharp smell of pine needles cling to everyone. Someone holds the lantern, and all I can see is a pile of sticks. Least that's what they look like to me. Morris says soon they're gonna look like letters, and those letters will spell out words.

He takes some sticks and makes a shape that looks like a hat. Says it's called an *A*. He makes two noises and says, "Those are the sounds *A* makes."

We smile at each other when we make the sounds, 'cause if anyone heard us they would swear there were voices coming from a grave, with all the *aaays* and *aaahhhs*. But we remember to keep real quiet.

Touch it," Morris says. "So you remember with your eyes, your ears, and your hands."

Doesn't make much sense to me, but I touch the sticks and try to remember the letter *A*. He scratches other letters out in the dirt. We do a lot of scratching to see if we can make the letters too.

"Y'all got to learn fast," Morris says. "Sun'll be on us before you know it."

A, *B*, and *C*. So many sounds and shapes in my head. I hope I can make room for all the other letters he says are coming. He's gonna teach us the whole alf-i-bet.

Master says slaves are too dumb to learn. You wouldn't know it, 'cause in this school, they are taking in learning like it's their last breath.

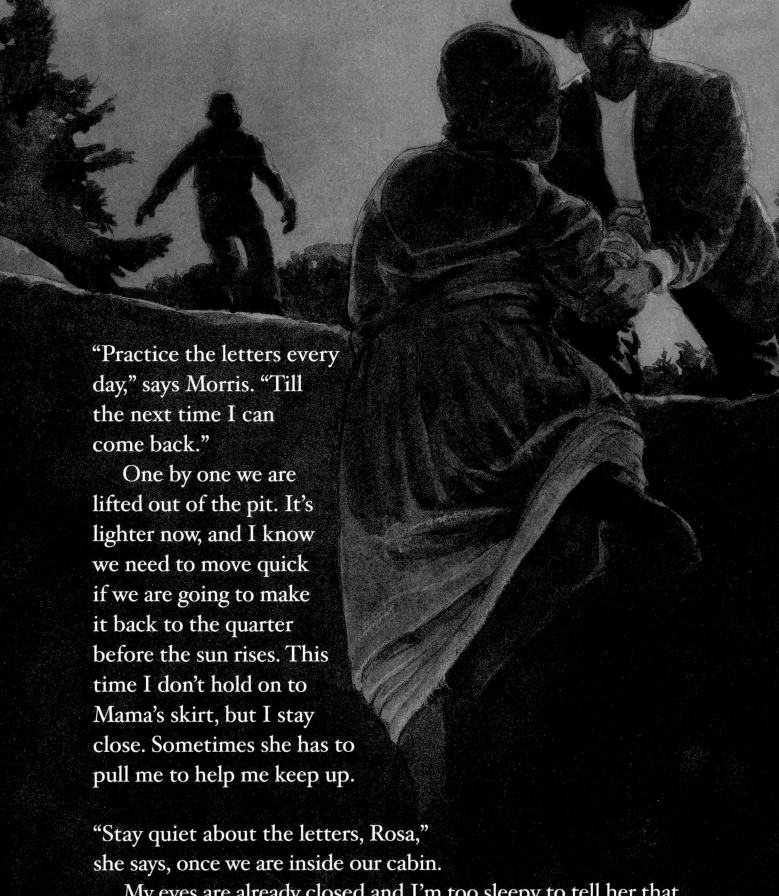

"Practice the letters every day," says Morris. "Till the next time I can come back."

One by one we are lifted out of the pit. It's lighter now, and I know we need to move quick if we are going to make it back to the quarter before the sun rises. This time I don't hold on to Mama's skirt, but I stay close. Sometimes she has to pull me to help me keep up.

"Stay quiet about the letters, Rosa," she says, once we are inside our cabin.

My eyes are already closed and I'm too sleepy to tell her that it won't be hard to keep our secret, 'cause all I need to do is think about the whip.

When the day starts I am so tired I hardly want to take care of the young'uns. But thinking about the letters keeps me awake.

I hear the letters when the young'uns call "Rosa!" And I hear them when I call my own mama. All day long they are in my head, safe from Master.

We can't go every night. Mama says it's too dangerous. But she always seems to know when it is time for school. Sometimes she just wakes me up, puts a finger to my lips, and we slip out. The crickets are so loud you can hardly hear the sticks cracking under our feet. It's better that way, 'cause no one wants to be caught out of the quarter.

Sometimes the patrollers ride all night, trying to find slaves who are away from their plantations or running to freedom. I hear they are like wolves—they see better at night. Lord help you if they catch you.

After a few more nights of lessons, I am aching. I know we're supposed to be quiet as cotton when we're walking, but I can't help asking Mama, "When are we gonna learn to read?"

Can't see her face well enough to know if she's mad, but her voice sounds tired. "Patience, Rosa," she says so low I can barely hear her. "There are folks a lot older than you who still can't read."

I look at my feet when I think about how long Mama's been waiting.

Our next night in school, we hear something outside. Hoofbeats. Maybe someone told the patrollers we were meeting. Might be they're looking for a runaway. Cold sweat and scared breath fill the pit. The rumble of the horses gets closer. Someone kneels to pray. I grab Mama's hand so hard she makes a face.

The horses stop above us, and so does our breathing.

Feels like I can't make my body hold still anymore. If we wait much longer, the sun'll be up.

"Let's try over by Ramsey's farm," a man says finally, close enough so we can hear. "Ain't nothing here."

The hoofbeats start to move away. One by one we all start breathing.

Morris says we may need to move the school or wait a while before we meet again.

The next day we hear two field hands talking. "The patrollers caught two of 'em coming back early in the morning. Their massa whipped 'em so bad, one of 'em near bleed to death." Mama's body gets as hard as wood.

Ain't no one gonna come to school now. Folks just too scared or just too tired of trying.

Days pass, and still no school. I've learned all my letters and I'm ready to make words. Morris told me after the letters comes the reading and writing.

Finally one night I can't wait any longer. I shake Mama.

"Not tonight, Rosa. It's still not safe."

I shake her again and don't stop till I feel her get up from her pallet. We leave for school under a speck of moonlight.

Morris is alone. Only me and Mama came to school.

As he helps us down, he smiles at me. "Didn't expect to see y'all tonight.

"Might as well get started," he says, and reaches for the stick. "Rosa, I got a word just for you." He writes four letters in the dirt, and I move closer to see.

"R-O-"

We hear them again. Footsteps this time, soft-like but sure. Like they know just where we are. Whispers and more steps. I look up at Mama, but she just stares at the roof. Master will whip us all, and Morris the most for teaching us. A lash for each letter.

And then there's another sound. Like the soft call of a bird. Morris reaches up to pull apart the branches. I raise the lantern to see who found us.

I see faces looking down at us, some I know and some I don't, but everyone waiting to step in. Into school.

We lift our arms to help one down and then the next. A girl, new and bigger than me, stands in the corner of the pit.

"Here," I say, picking up a stick. "I'll show you how I write my name."

Author's Note

Years ago, while combing through research for a picture book I was writing about Frederick Douglass, I came across a passage about pit schools. Pit schools, I discovered, were essentially large holes dug deep in the ground and disguised with sticks and branches. In the dark of night, slaves would slip away from their plantations and meet at "school" to learn to read and write from another, literate slave.

The knowledge that slaves would go to these lengths to learn to read evoked in me profound pain, respect, and awe.

Like Frederick Douglass, these slaves risked their lives to learn, trading injury and sometimes even death for letters and words.

This book is a celebration of those who sought the light of knowledge during the darkness of slavery.

"Once you learn to read, you will be forever free."
—Frederick Douglass

Further Reading

Cline-Ransome, Lesa. *Words Set Me Free: The Story of Young Frederick Douglass.* New York: Simon & Schuster, 2012.

Douglass, Frederick. *Narrative of the Life of Frederick Douglass, an American Slave.* New York: Barnes & Noble Books, 2003.

Paulsen, Gary. *Nightjohn.* New York: Laurel Leaf, 1995.

Text copyright © 2013 by Lesa Cline-Ransome

Illustrations copyright © 2013 by James E. Ransome

First Edition
1 3 5 7 9 10 8 6 4 2
F850-6835-5-12288

Library of Congress Cataloging-in-Publication Data

Cline-Ransome, Lesa.
  Light in the darkness : a story about how slaves learned in secret / by Lesa Cline-Ransome ; illustrations by James E. Ransome. — 1st ed.
     p. cm.
  Summary: Risking a whipping if they are discovered, Rosa and her mama sneak away from their slave quarters during the night to a hidden location in a field where they learn to read and write in a pit school.
  ISBN 978-1-4231-3495-4
[1. Reading—Fiction. 2. Learning—Fiction. 3. Slavery—Fiction. 4. African Americans—Fiction. 5. Southern States—History—1775–1865—Fiction.] I. Ransome, James, ill. II. Title.
  PZ7.C622812Lig 2013
  [E]—dc23   2012001834

This book is set in Hoefler Text.
Designed by Tyler Nevins
Printed in Singapore
Reinforced binding
Visit www.disneyhyperionbooks.com